Our Little Spanish Cousin

Mary F. Nixon-Roulet

Our Little Spanish Cousin

CHAPTER I.

THE CHRISTENING

ONE of the first things which Fernando remembered was the christening of his little sister. He was five years old and had no other brother or sister to play with, for Pablo, his wonderful big brother, was away at the Naval School, and his older sister, Augustia, was at school in the convent.

When Fernando's nurse told him that he had a little sister he was delighted, and begged to see her; and when all his relatives on both sides of the house came to see the baby christened, he was still more pleased.

Fernando was a little Spanish boy, and in his country a great deal is thought of kinsfolk, for the Spanish are very warm-hearted and affectionate. So Fernando was glad to see all his aunts and uncles and cousins and all the friends who happened to be visiting them at the time.

Fernando's father, the Señor Don Juan de Guzman, was a courtly gentleman, and he bowed low over the ladies' hands, and said, "The house is yours, señora!" to each one; so, as boys generally copy their fathers, Fernando assured his little cousins that he "placed himself at their feet," and welcomed them just as politely as his father had the older folk.

What a wonderful time he had that day! First came the christening in the great Cathedral which towers above Granada, and in which lie buried the king and queen, Ferdinand and Isabella, in whose reign Columbus sailed away from Spain to discover America. The Cathedral was so grand that it always made Fernando feel very strange and quiet, and he thought it was shocking that the baby cried when the priest poured water on her and baptized her, Maria Dolores Concepcion Isabel Inez Juanita. This seems a long name for such a tiny little mite, but there was a reason for every single name, and not one could be left out. Nearly all Spanish children are named Maria, whether boys or girls, because the Spaniards are devoted to the Virgin Mary, and as the baby was born on the Feast of the Immaculate Conception, she was called Concepcion. Isabel was for her aunt, and Inez was for her godmother, and Juanita for her father. Her name did not seem at all long to Fernando, for his name was Fernando Antonio Maria Allegria Francisco Ruy Guzman y Ximenez. Every one called him Fernando or Nando, and his long name had troubled him but once in all his gay little life. That time he had been naughty and had run away from his aya, the nurse who always watches little Spanish children like a faithful dog, and he had fallen into the deep ditch beside the great aloe hedge.

The aloes are stalwart plants with long leaves, wide-extending and saw-toothed, and they are often planted close together so as to make hedgerows through which cattle cannot pass. The leaves of the aloe are sometimes a yard long, and they are very useful. From them are made strong cords, and also the alpagatas, or sandals, which the peasants wear; and the fibres of the leaf are separated from the pulp and made into many things to wear. The central stem of the aloe grows sometimes twenty feet high, and it has a number of stems on the ends of which grow yellow flowers. The leaves are a bluish-green in colour, and look like long blue swords. The long hedgerows look very beautiful against the soft blue of the Spanish sky, but little Fernando did not see anything pretty in them as he lay at the bottom of the ditch, roaring lustily.

"Who's there?" demanded an American gentleman, who was travelling in Spain, as he came along on the other side of the hedge, and Fernando replied, "Fernando Antonio Maria Allegria Francisco Ruy Guzman y Ximenez!"

"If there's so many of you I should think you could help each other out," said the American, and when he finally extricated one small boy he laughed heartily, and said, as he took Fernando home:

"I should think a name like that would topple you over." After that Fernando always called Americans "the people who laugh."

After the baby was christened, they went home through the narrow streets of the quaint old town. All the horses wore bells, and, as they trotted along, the tinkle, tinkle sounded like sleighing-time in America. The reason for this is that in many places the streets are too narrow for two carriages to pass, and the bells give warning that a vehicle is coming, so that the one coming from the opposite direction may find a wide spot in the road, and there wait till the other carriage has passed.

As the christening party went toward the home of Fernando, it passed a man driving two or three goats, and he stopped in front of a house, from a window of which was let down a string and a pail. Into this the man looked, and taking out a piece of money which lay in the bottom, he milked the pail full from one of the goats, and the owner pulled it up to her window again. It seems a strange way to get your morning's milk, but it is sure to be fresh and sweet, right from the goat, and there is no chance to put water in it, as milkmen sometimes do in America.

The houses Fernando passed were all painted in many soft colours, and they had charming little iron balconies, to some of which palm branches were fastened, blessed palms from the church at Holy Week, which the Spaniards believe will keep lightning from striking the house.

Fernando's house was much larger than the rest, for his father was a noble of one of the oldest families in Spain, whose ancestors had done many splendid things for the state in the olden times. The house had several balconies, from which hung down long sprays of blossoms, for every balcony railing was filled with flower-pots. There grew vines and flowers, nasturtiums, hyacinths, wallflowers, pinks and violets, their sweet scents filling the air.

When the christening party entered the house, the baby was borne off to the nursery, and Fernando, no longer a baby, but a big boy with a baby sister, was allowed to go with the rest to the patio, where breakfast was served.

The patio is one of the most charming things about the real Spanish houses. It is a court in the centre of the house, larger than an ordinary room, with a marble floor and a huge awning which protects from the sun, yet leaves the patio open to the fresh air and sweet scents of the sunny out-of-doors. All the family gather in the patio, and it is the favourite lounging-place for old and young. In the patioof the Señor Guzman's house were orange-trees and jasmine, and all colours of violets bloomed around the marble rim of the fountain, which was in the centre.

What a wonderful thing that christening feast was to Fernando! There was much laughing and talking, and such good things to eat!

When all were through eating, little Juanita's health was drunk, and her godfather proposed her health, and recited a poem he had composed in her honour.

"Queridita Ahijada!

Plague alecielo qui tu vida

Sea feliz y placentera

Cual arroyo cristalino

Qui atra viesa la pradera

Su Padrino, Francesco."

This very much delighted every one, and so with laughter and merriment the christening feast was over.

CHAPTER II.

SCHOOL-DAYS

WHEN Fernando was seven years old he began to go to school. Little Juanita cried bitterly, for she was devoted to the big brother who played such lovely games with her, and she did not like to think of his being away from her nearly all day. However, she was told that Fernando was a big boy now, and that before long she would be having a governess to teach her to read and embroider, so she stopped crying very quickly, for she was a sunny little child, and went to picking flowers in the garden quite contentedly.

How grown up Fernando felt! To be a real schoolboy! His school-days were all alike. He arose at half-past seven, when the church-bells were ringing for the daily service; he had a bath, said his prayers, and dressed himself very neatly, for he had first to be looked over by his aya, and then inspected by his mamma, to see if he could pass muster, and was clean and neat as a little Spanish gentleman should be. Mamma being satisfied with his appearance, he gave her his morning kiss, and greeted the rest of the family. Then followed breakfast,—a simple, wholesome meal of semula, or gruel and warm milk, with bread and honey and eggs.

After a run in the garden, the ayo, or preceptor, called to take him to school. Fernando skipped happily away to study until twelve o'clock, when dinner was served to the day boarders, a dinner of soup, vegetables, and dessert, with a little playtime afterward. Spanish boys do not take tea or coffee until they are grown up. At half-past four the boys are turned out of school, and then comes the delight of the day to Fernando. His ayo has disappeared, and in his stead has come Manuel, his own man, who tells such delightful stories of knights and warriors and the glories of Spain, and who thinks that all his little master does is perfect. Manuel knows all about the city, and he is willing to take Fernando any place he wishes to go, provided it is a fit place for a boy of rank. He knows just where the marionettes are playing, and if there is a gay crowd on the square, a trained bear or a funny little monkey, he will be sure to have heard about it, and take Fernando to see it. If there is no special excitement, Manuel takes him to the paseo, where all the boys of the town gather. Here they play in mimic battles and bull-fights, and Fernando enters into everything with delight, until Manuel thinks it is time for the señora, his mother, to pass by in the carriage. How delighted the little boy is to see her, and how his tongue rattles as he tells her all the events of the day, as he rides home with her through the long soft twilight of the soft Spanish night! How good his supper tastes, a simple little supper of chocolate, rich and dark, white bread and golden honey, with some little iced cakes, which dear old Dolores, the cook, has made for the little master. All the servants love Fernando dearly, for though he has a hot temper, and sometimes is very wilful, he is so loving that they do not mind his naughtiness. After supper Fernando says the rosary with his aya, goes over his lessons a little, and then tumbles into bed in a happy slumber.

All his days are very much alike, for Spanish children are brought up very simply, and have little excitement, though they have many pleasures. There are little visits paid to aunts and cousins, visits remembered not too pleasantly by the pet dog and parrot of his aunt. The parrot was brought from Cuba by Uncle Enrico, the priest. The bird knows Fernando well, and scolds terribly in most unchurchly language every time he approaches the cage. The French poodle, too, does not greatly care for a visit from Fernando, for the boy cannot help teasing, and the fat, stupid dog, his Aunt Isabel's darling, does nothing but lie around on silken cushions and eat comfits. Fernando likes animals, and would never really hurt one, but there is something in the calm self-satisfaction of Beppino which stirs up all the mischief in him, and Aunt Isabel has been heard to exclaim: "Fernando will be my death! He is a dear boy, and if it came to choosing between him and Beppo, I am quite sure that I would take my nephew, but, thank Heaven, I have not to choose!"

Fernando's own dog was different. He found him one day close by the garden railing, a poor, ragged fellow, lean and hungry, with a lame foot, but a pair of pleading and wistful brown eyes, which, with all their misery, had yet a look of good-fellowship within them which appealed to Fernando's gay nature, as the pitiful plight of the little fellow appealed to his tender heart. The dog put a pink tongue through the railing and licked Fernando's hand, and that clinched the bargain. Henceforth the two were friends. Fernando persuaded Manuel to bathe and tie up the wounded foot, and feed the puppy. That was all the boy dared at first, but the next day he found the dog in the same place and fed him again. Every day after that the little tramp followed him to school, and when school was over his yellow-haired dogship awaited his benefactor. Manuel winked at the friendship, and allowed Mazo, as Fernando called him, to have many a good meal at the garden gate. Manuel was a great stickler for the proprieties, but he had been a boy once, and there were some things that Fernando's lady mother would not at all have comprehended, that good old Manuel understood perfectly. Mazo was far more interesting to Fernando than the thoroughbred, ladylike pets of his mother, and it was a sore subject with him that Mazo, who was so clever, who could whip the tramp dogs of any of his school friends, should be kept outside the house. His mother did not seem to realize that Mazo's fighting qualities were what made him valuable. One fatal day, when she had driven to the paseo a little earlier than usual, and had seen a fight between Mazo and another little dog, equally disreputable, she had cried out:

"Fernando, come away from that ferocious beast! He must be mad!" and she had seemed anything but reassured when Fernando had tried to calm her by saying:

"But, mamma, he is not mad; I know him well; he is the gentlest of beings, and he can whip any dog in the paseo," the pride of possession getting the better of prudence.

Thereafter Manuel was most careful of Mazo's appearance. He captured him and washed him, and let him sleep in a shed at night, and by degrees the little fellow lost his trampish appearance, and became a semi-respectable member of society, though still ready to follow Fernando like a shadow, to fight at his will, and to share with him an excursion into forbidden lands. It was really droll to see the different airs which Mazo could assume. He had ever an eye upon his audience, having early learned in the hard school of misfortune that his comfort depended not at all upon himself, but upon the humour of those about him. With the outside world his look was wary. With the family of his master he was apologetic. His brown eye seemed to say: "I place myself at your feet, most noble señors; I pray you excuse me for living." But with Fernando, while it was tempered with respect, his air was one of good-fellowship alone. Even the señora herself, the head of the house and authority in chief, as is the case in all Spanish households, came to regard Fernando's dog with a degree of friendliness, and finding this out, the servants treated him kindly, and Mazo decided that his lines had fallen in pleasant places. Upon this, however, he never presumed. He knew not how long it would last, but felt that he was upon good behaviour. He restrained his desire to chase Juanita's pet cat, and to bark when the parrot imitated his barking, though the restraint put upon himself must have been severe, for he made up for it when out with Manuel and Fernando. Then he was himself again, Mazo the tramp.

CHAPTER III.

A VISIT TO A HACIENDA

ONE day in October, when the sun was shining in golden beauty, the señora said to her husband:

"I should like to go to the hacienda to-morrow, and take the children with me, for la niña has never seen the picking, and Fernando did not go last year or the year before."

"It will give me pleasure to escort you," said the Señor de Guzman, in the courtly manner which Spanish gentlemen use toward their wives. "At what hour will it please you to start?"

"As early as you can," she answered. "So that we may arrive there in plenty of time to see the picking before luncheon, and after asiesta, drive back in the pleasant part of the afternoon."

"We shall start at nine, then," said her husband, "and should arrive there by ten or a little after."

When Fernando returned from school and heard that he was to accompany his mother next day, he was nearly beside himself with joy.

"Juanita," he cried, "you have no idea how delightful it is at the fruit farm! I have not been there for two years, but I remember it well. All the oranges one can eat, and such raisins! You will much enjoy it, I am sure."

He was up bright and early next day, and impatient to start long before his mother was ready, and even his father was waiting before the señora made her appearance. She was a large woman, and very slow and graceful in her movements. No one had ever seen herhurried, and every one expected to wait for her, so that it was nearly half-past nine when they started. The coachman whipped up the horses, and away they went skimming over the rough stones. Fernando sat with Diego and Manuel on the front seat of the carriage, while Dolores sat beside the señora, holding Juanita on her lap. The señor rode upon his high-stepping Andalusian horse beside the carriage, and pointed out places of interest to the children as they drove along.

A gay young officer passed by them, young and slim, riding a handsome horse, and some soldiers were manœuvring on the Plaza. One poor fellow, once a gay soldier, but now with an empty sleeve, dressed in a faded army blouse and wearing a merit medal, was begging in the street, and the señor stopped to give him a piece of silver, for Spaniards are always generous and pitiful, and cannot resist a beggar. "He had served in Cuba," said the señor to his wife, and she sighed as she thought of the many lost to Spain and their dear ones in that useless war.

Fruit-venders passed along the street, and donkeys so laden with fruit and flowers that almost nothing could be seen of them but their slim little legs and their great waving ears. Water-carriers were there, carrying huge jars which looked like those used by the old Moors; and a travelling merchant, in gray garments, but with brightly dressed mules. It was not so bright a party that they passed later, for a peasant funeral passed by on its way to the cemetery. Four young men carried the bier, upon which was the body of a child, covered all but its face, which lay exposed to the sun.

"Take off your hat, son," said the señora. "Always do so to a passing funeral, for maybe yours will be the last salute the dead will receive on earth."

No sooner was the funeral passed than there came a straw and charcoal merchant, crying, "Paja! Carbon! Cabrito!" So many people in Granada have no way to warm themselves except by the brazero, in which charcoal is burnt, that there is great need for the charcoal man, and he drives a brisk trade.

Next they saw a priest on a sick call, for he bore the Blessed Sacrament. A crowd of ragged urchins stopped in their play to kneel as he passed, and Fernando and his father raised their hats.

By this time, the carriage had reached the outskirts of the city, and the road wound along the banks of the Darro, a rushing stream which gushes out of a deep mountain gorge, and passes through the town. Its banks are lined with quaint old houses, leaning far over the river, and Fernando saw women there, washing their linen in the water, and spreading their clothes on the stones to dry.

Outside of the town their way lay along the beautiful Vega, which stretches beyond Granada, in green and fertile loveliness, to the far-away hills. Crossed by two rivers, the Darro and Genil, the plain is dotted with whitewashed villas, nestling like birds in the soft green of the olive and orange trees. Sloping gradually to the mountains above, the Vega is green as emerald, and truly a fair sight beneath the turquoise sky, and the mother-of-pearl of the snowy mountains.

Fernando's father owned large estates upon the hillsides, and raised oranges and grapes. The last were used for raisins, the grapes from which the finest wine is made, the Amontillado, for which Spain is so famous, not reaching their greatest perfection in this part of the land.

In an hour they reached the farm and drove down the long lane which led to the house. The Hacienda of Santa Eulalia was a large, low building, with a broad porch and a tangle of vines and roses climbing over it. Huge trees spread their arms over the roof, and from the balcony one could see groves of cypress-trees, pines, oaks, and poplars, beyond the fruit-trees, and, above all, the rose-coloured peaks of the Sierras. Upon the slope of the hill, as it fell away toward Granada, were the grape-vines, with huge clusters of grapes, purple, white, and red, weighing down the vines. There were, too, terraces where the raisins dried; and nearer the house were the drying-sheds, where an army of packers pressed the raisins under boards, and carefully sorted them before packing. The vineyards were beautiful, but even more so were the orange groves, and one who has seen a grove in full fruit never forgets the beautiful sight. The trees are deep green in colour, and full of leaves, many of them bearing at the same time flowers and green and ripe fruit.

The children were wild with delight, and ran about eager to see the picking and sorting of the fine fruit, for the oranges of Santa Eulalia were famous for size and quality. The trees grew rather low to the ground, and were covered with fruit which the pickers were gathering. Ladders were put up to the lower branches, and each picker carried a basket swung to his neck by a cord. He carefully picked the oranges, one at a time, and dropped them in his basket, and so expert were many of them that it seemed as if they had scarcely mounted the ladder before the basket was full. Many young girls were employed as pickers, and they were particularly skilful, vying with the men in their swiftness. Very gay were their voices, and merry jest and song enlivened the work, until it seemed as if it were not work but play. Fernando and Juanita hopped about like little rabbits, eating the fruit which rolled to the ground, for often the golden globes fell from the trees, as they were shaken by the picking.

When the baskets were filled, the oranges were carried to the sheds and left overnight to harden the skins a little, when each orange was wrapped in soft tissue-paper. For this are employed young boys and girls, and very expert they grow in the wrapping of the oranges, each one being properly wrapped with but a twist of the hand. The next thing is the packing, and the oranges are stored away in wooden boxes, and are ready to be shipped to market.

The children ate so many oranges that they scarcely wanted any of the luncheon prepared for them at the hacienda. There was an omelet with green peppers, a delicious salad, some fowl, and tiny round potato balls, all sprinkled over with chopped parsley, with a huge dish of oranges and grapes for dessert.

The señora insisted upon a little siesta after luncheon, but Fernando's eyes were so wide open that he could not close them as he swung to and fro in the great hammock between two orange-trees in front of the house. He was delighted when his father sat down beside him, in one of the big easy chairs, and said:

"You look to me like a boy who would like to hear a story."

"Indeed I would; please tell me one," said Fernando.

"Have you ever heard about the judges of Pedro the Cruel?"

"No, papa," said Fernando, all interest.

"A long time ago, there ruled over Andalusia a king named Pedro, and he was so disliked by his subjects, and did so many wicked things, that he was called Pedro the Cruel. He lived in the city of Sevilla, and though he was cruel, and often heartless, still he had a strong sense of justice, which would not allow the common people to be badly treated. He found out one day that four of his judges had been cheating the people and taking bribes, and he determined to teach them a lesson. He went to his favourite gardens, those of the Alcazar, and sent for the judges to come to him there. It is a wonderful place even to-day, and then it must have been very beautiful. Huge banana-trees waved their rough green leaves above the tangled beauty of the flower-beds, where jasmine and violets and roses grew in profusion. In the midst was a fountain, and Don Pedro knelt beside it, smiling wickedly as he placed upon the perfumed waters, five oranges cut in halves, and placed flat-side down. The reflection was so perfect that any one would be deceived, and think they were whole oranges floating upon the water.

"'How many oranges are there here?' asked the king, smiling genially, and the judges replied:

"'Ten, may it please your Gracious Majesty.'

"'Nay, but it does not please my Gracious Majesty to have four fools for judges,' he said. 'Liars! Can you not see that there are but five?' and he raised two of the halves and held them together. 'Know, oh, unjust judges,' he said, sternly, 'that the king's servants must see more than the surface of things if they are to conduct that portion of the realm which it is their business to attend to, and since you cannot tell a half from a whole, perchance that is the reason of the tales I hear of your ill-dealings with the property of some of my subjects!'

"He ordered them to be beheaded and their places filled with better men, and the poor people whom they had defrauded had their property restored to them. There are many other stories of King Pedro which are not pleasant to tell, and it is good to remember that he sometimes did kind things."

"Thank you," said Fernando. "What is the Alcazar where the gardens were?"

"It is a very remarkable place, and when you go to Sevilla you will see it. At first, hundreds of years ago, when the Romans were in Spain, it was the house of Cæsar; afterward the Moors turned it into a fortress, and it is a perfect example of Moorish work. Don Pedro rebuilt it, and spent a great deal of money upon it, making it the most beautiful palace in all Spain. All manner of things happened there, among them the murder of Don Pedro's half-brother, Don Fadrique, who he was afraid would lay claim to the throne.

"But here come your mother and Juanita, and I think your rest time is about over. Go and play, and tell Manuel we return at four o'clock, so you must be on time."

So Fernando spent a delightful afternoon in the orange grove, and drove home through the cool twilight, passing the paseo just as the band was playing the Marche Real, the national song, which he hummed until he went to bed.

CHAPTER IV.

AT THE ALHAMBRA

"Mi madre," cried Fernando, rushing into the house one day in October, "to-day is the feast-day of the head master, and we have a holiday. May I have permission to go to the hill to see Antonio?"

"Not by yourself, my son," replied his mother, and Fernando said, hastily, "Oh, no, madre mia, Manuel says that he will take me if you will permit me, and, if Juanita's nurse could be spared, we could take the niña, as she has never been there, and that would give her pleasure."

"Let me see," his mother paused a moment, "the day is fine. This morning I am busy, but after luncheon I will drive thither with thelittle one, and leave you for an hour while I go on to the villa of the Señora Sanchez; but you must be a good boy, and mind Manuel."

"Yes, mother, and you will see Antonio, whom I like best of all the boys at school," said Fernando, and he hastened away to make ready for the great treat. A drive with his mother in school hours was a pleasure seldom indulged in, and a visit to the great hill which crowns Granada was treat enough, but to take Juanita,—these were things so pleasant that he said to himself, "I think my guardian angel must have whispered in my mother's ear to give me all this pleasure."

It was about two o'clock as they drove through the narrow streets of the city up the steep and hilly way which led to the outskirts of the town.

"You are going to see the nicest boy in Granada, and the most wonderful castle in Spain, niña," said Fernando to Juanita, and the two children chattered merrily as the carriage went slowly up the hill.

"Here is a riddle I heard at school, niña, see if you can guess it,—

"'Guarded in a prison strait,

Ivory gaolers round her wait,

Venomous snake of sanguine hue,

Mother of all the lies that brew!'"

"I do not know," said his little sister, wonderingly. She thought all that Fernando said and did was perfection. "What is it, Nando?"

"Why, the tongue, of course," he said, pleased to have given a riddle which she could not guess; and his mother said:

"That is a very good riddle, and I hope you will remember it, for it is the tongue which makes much mischief in this world. Remember that 'a stone and a word flung do not return.'"

"There is Mazo following us," said Juanita, and her mother said, laughingly, "Really, Fernando, I don't see why you like that dog so much! He is uglier than Picio."

"He isn't handsome, but you have told me that handsome is as handsome does!" said her son, and his mother laughed again.

"Oh, what is that?" cried Juanita, as the carriage made a turn, and some splendid great towers came into view.

"That is the Alhambra," said Fernando. "It is the most wonderful castle in Spain. Manuel said it was begun in 1238, in the reign of the Moorish king, Ibn-l-Ahmar, and it was years and years in building. He says the Moors used to have the castle and the city of Granada, and I read in my history of how the Catholic king, Ferdinand, came here to conquer it. He fought and fought, but the Moors wouldn't give it up. I think they were a brave people, if they were beaten, don't you?"

"Yes, my son, they were very brave, but they did such cruel things to the captives they took, that it is not surprising that the Spaniards wanted to conquer them," said his mother.

"They captured Christian girls, and forced them to become their wives, though what they wanted with them I cannot see, for they already had many wives, and I should think one was enough for any man. Where shall we find your friend, Fernando? If you wish I will leave you with him for an hour, and continue my drive."

"Oh, thank you, mother, I knew you would let me stay!" cried Fernando; and Juanita said, "Please leave me, too, mother, that I may see Antonio and the great palace."

"Antonio lives within the palace, mamma," said Fernando. "He was born there, and he and his sister, Pepita, have never been away. He is to go to the English school at Gibraltar, but not until he is bigger. May we ask some one where he is?"

"Certainly. He must be a nice boy to have lived always in such a place, and to have you so devoted to him. There is a guard; ask him where the apartments of the boy's father are," she said to Manuel, who sat upon the box with the coachman. Further inquiry, however, was not necessary, for, as the carriage made its way up the broad drive shaded with magnificent elm-trees, which the Duke of Wellington planted, a boy came bounding toward them.

"There he is," cried Fernando. "Antonio, come here, we have come to see you."

The carriage stopped, and Fernando hopped out as lightly as a squirrel, giving Antonio a good hug, for Spanish boys are never ashamed of showing that they like their friends. Antonio's cap was off in a trice and he smiled and bowed as Fernando presented him to his mother and little sister. Antonio was a handsome boy, with eyes as dark and blue as the sapphire of the Spanish skies, and fair hair tossed back from an open brow. All Spaniards are not dark, and, in Andalusia, the province in which Granada lies, there are many blonds.

"I will leave Fernando and Juanita with you for a visit," said the señora, graciously. "Will you bring them here in an hour?"

"Si, señora," said Antonio. "But if you would so honour us, the señora, my mother has prepared a little luncheon in the Garden of Lindaraya at four o'clock, and she would be most happy if you would partake of it with us."

"Thank you, then I shall allow the children to remain with you until that time and I shall myself prolong my visit with my friends at the villa," she replied. "When I return I shall do myself the pleasure of meeting your mother."

So she drove off, and the children tripped happily away, followed closely by Manuel and Dolores, for Spanish little ones of good family are never allowed to go about alone. However, one must relax a little sometimes, and the two attendants saw a pleasant hour before them as they sat idly about while the children played in the wonderful gardens of the palace. Pepita, Antonio's sister, was but a year older than Juanita, and the two little girls were quite happy together, and the boys did not consider themselves too big to play with them. They played hide and seek through the marble halls, and tag and chaser about the flower beds. The little girls played house and made mud pies, although Dolores objected to this and told Juanita that she would be as dirty as the "caseada de Burguillos" if she were not more careful. Juanita thought Pepita was wonderfulbecause she had been born in a palace, and her father was custodian of the wonderful place, but it was Antonio who claimed her greatest admiration. He was even more marvellous than Fernando, she almost thought, because he was bigger, and his eyes had such a kind and merry look, and he always carried her over the rough places in his strong young arms, and lifted her over the walls as they strolled through the gardens.

She had never seen such gardens as these of the Alhambra. They were full of the most beautiful flowers, and there was the most delicious scent in the air.

Antonio told her it was from the wallflowers, which grew here in great profusion, and were twice as large as they were in other places. But besides them there were great trees of purple heliotrope, the blooms as large around as Juanita's big hat; and geranium-trees, taller than a man, with orange-trees in bloom, late though it was, and with the ripe fruit upon their branches also.

Then the children had a charming luncheon on the grass, for Antonio's mother set forth for them all manner of good things, — a dainty salad with some cold meat, thick chocolate in tiny cups, and cakes in the daintiest of shapes. What a merry picnic it was beneath the shade of the great orange-tree which Antonio told them had been there for over a hundred years, and from which the great American, Washington Irving, had picked fruit when he lived at the Alhambra! Then when the party was over, and his mother had not come, Fernando said:

"Antonio, tell us a story. You know some about the castle, I am sure." And little Juanita begged, "Do please tell us one, Antonio," and as nobody could ever resist the niña's wistful, brown eyes, Antonio smilingly began the story of "The Three Sisters."

CHAPTER V.

ANTONIO'S STORY

"ONCE upon a time," Antonio began, "there were in the palace of the Alhambra three princesses whose names were Zayde, Zorayde and Zorahayda. They were daughters of the Sultan, for it was in the days when the Moors reigned in Granada, and there were no Christians here but captive Spaniards. The princesses were kept in a tower called the Tower of the Infantas, one of the most beautiful towers of the Alhambra. It was fitted up in a manner befitting the home of the king's daughters. The walls of the room were hung with tapestries in cloth of gold and royal blue; the divans were heaped high with pillows, the pillars and arches which held up the roof itself,were in filigree of softest hues,—blue, terra-cotta, and gold. The Princess Zayde's chamber was the richest, all in cloth of gold, since she was the eldest Infanta; that of Zorayde was hung with steel mirrors, burnished bright, for she was most fair to look upon and loved to look upon herself; while that of the youngest, little brown-eyed Princess Zorahayda, was delicate in tone, as if some rare jewel lay in a dainty casket. Upon the princesses waited the discreet Kadiga, an elderly duenna who never let them from her sight for a moment. She watched them as a cat does a mouse, but there was one thing she could not control, and that was the eyes of the princesses. They would look forth from the windows, and, indeed, this Kadiga never forbade, for it seemed to her a pity that three such fair maidens should have so little amusement, and she thought it could not possibly hurt them to gaze into the gardens below.

"One day, while the princesses were looking out the narrow windows, they saw something which made them look and look again. Yes, it was true,—could it be? it was! They were the very same—the three Christian princes whom they had seen at Salobrena; but here they were labouring as captives. At the tourney to which the princesses had been taken, they had seen these noble knights, and had fallen in love with them, and it was for this that their father had shut them up in a tower, for he had said no daughter of his should marry a Christian.

"But the knights thought differently, and they had come to Granada in the hope of finding their princesses, and had been taken captive and were compelled to hard labour.

"'It is he!' cried Zayde. 'The knight with the scarlet tunic is the one I saw!'

"'Yes, but the one in blue, he is mine!' cried Zorayde.

"Little Zorahayda said nothing, but she looked with all her eyes at the third knight. And this was not the last time she saw him, for the knights had come thither, bent on rescuing the maidens, and had bribed their jailer to help them to escape. So one moonlight night, when the moon was turning into silver beauty the orange-trees of the garden, and shining in fullest light into the deep ravine below the Tower of the Infantas, the knights awaited their lady-loves in the valley below, and Kadiga let them down by a rope-ladder.

"All escaped in safety but little Zorahayda, and she feared to go.

"'Leave me,' she cried. 'I must not leave my father!' and at last, since they could not persuade her to go, they rode sadly away without her, and her little white hand waved a sad farewell to them from the window. There she still is, so say the legends, and there are those who, walking in these gardens at midnight, tell that they have seen a white hand wave from the tower window, and a voice whisper through the murmur of the fountains, 'Ay di mi Zorahayda!'"

"Oh, Antonio! hast thou seen her?" cried Juanita, and her brother laughed, and said:

"Little foolish one, it is but a story! But Antonio, tell us a tale of battle, for this is but a woman's story, and there have been splendid deeds done in this old castle."

"Splendid ones, and sorry ones as well," said Antonio, who was old for his twelve years, and had lived so long in the atmosphere of romance that he seemed a part of it, in speech and manners. "Shall I tell you of the taking of the Alhambra from the Moors? It was a glorious fight, and both sides were brave men."

Then he told them of the conquest of Granada, when Christian knight and Moor fought valiantly for the possession of the splendid city, with its gem, the Alhambra. He told of how the noble knight, Juan de Véga, was sent to demand tribute from Muley ben Hassan, King of Granada, and that fierce old monarch said:

"Return to your sovereigns, O Spaniard, and tell them that the kings of Granada who paid tribute are all dead. My mint coins only swords!" Brave words, but it was his son, Boabdil the Unlucky, who was forced to surrender the castle to the victorious enemy, and who handed the keys to the Spaniards, as he rode through the gate of the Siete Suelos, saying: "Go, possess these fortresses which Allah has taken from me, but grant me this one boon, that none other shall pass under this gateway from which I have come out." And Ferdinand granted his request and walled up the gate, so that, from that day to this, no one has passed through that entrance.

These and other tales Antonio told them, and the afternoon passed so quickly that the children were surprised when their mother's voice warned them that it was time to go home.

"Oh, mamma," they cried, "must we go?" and the señora smilingly waited a little, chatting with Antonio's mother, while he picked a huge bunch of flowers for the children to carry away with them. Then the good-byes were said, and they drove away crying:

"Come soon to see us, Antonio." To which he replied, in pleasant Spanish fashion:

"Thank you well, and very much for your visit!"

"Isn't he a nice boy?" said Juanita.

"Quite a little Don," her mother answered, smiling. "Fernando, I am glad to see that you have the sense to choose your friends so well," and Fernando grinned, boylike, well pleased.

"Oh, who is that?" Juanita asked, as a fantastic figure approached.

"That is the gipsy king," said her mother. "You know the gipsies live all huddled together there, below the Alhambra, and they have a chief whom they call king. They are a lazy set, doing little but thieving and telling fortunes. They live in little burrows, like rabbits, set into the hillsides, and there are pigs, goats, and dogs all living together with the people."

"That girl with the king is very pretty," said Fernando, "with her black hair and eyes, and her bright skirts, and the pomegranate flower behind her ear."

"The pomegranate is the flower of Granada, you know," said his mother, "and it does look pretty in her dark hair. Hear her call her dogs! Gipsy dogs are all named Melampo, Cubilon, or Lubina, after the shepherd dogs who followed the shepherds, and saw our Lord at Bethlehem. Ah, Juanita, 'Jesus, Maria y Josef!' You must not sneeze! Drive faster, Diego, and Dolores, wrap the baby in that Palencian blanket, so soft and warm. The nights grow cool quickly at this time of year."

"Why do we always say 'Jesus, Maria y Josef!' when people sneeze?" asked Fernando.

"It has been the custom so long that people have almost forgotten why it is done," replied his mother; "but I remember my grandmother saying once that her mother told her the reason. Years and years ago, in 1580, there was in all Andalusia a terrible plague called themosquillo. People sneezed once, and lo! they had the plague, and little could save them, though some few recovered. So it grew to be the custom, when one sneezed, for those who heard him to look pityingly upon him and say, 'Dios le ayude,' or call upon the holy names to help him, saying, 'Jesus, Maria y Josef.'"

"See that ragged beggar, mamma," said Juanita. "May we not give him something?" as a little boy came hopping along beside the carriage, crying, lustily:

"Una limosna por el amor de Dios, señora!"

"I have no centimos," said the señora, "and it is not wise to give more to a beggar, but you can always give politeness, niña, and when you have no money say, 'Perdone me, usted,' or, 'Por el amor de Dios,' and thus you will not give offence to God's poor."

CHAPTER VI.

THE HOLIDAYS

FERNANDO had been three months in school and was beginning to grow tired, when it came time for the feast of Christmas, and he was very happy in the thought of all he was to do and see during his holiday. He and Juanita were very much excited in preparing theirnacimento, which nearly every Spanish child has at Christmas time. This is a plaster representation of the birth of Christ. There are in it many figures, a manger surrounded with greens, the Baby Our Lord, St. Joseph, and the Blessed Virgin, the Wise Men worshipping the Holy Child, and angels hovering near, as well as the patient ox and ass who were his first worshippers. Juanita was wild with excitement as these were all grouped and set in place. She was only four and did not well remember the Christmas before, so that it was all new to her.

Christmas Eve there was a grand family party, all the relatives coming to the home of Fernando and partaking of a supper of sweetmeats and wine. In the morning there was, of course, early Mass in the great cathedral, where the choir sang divinely. It started way up in the loft to sing the Adeste Fideles, the Church's Christmas hymn for centuries, slowly coming nearer and nearer; and Juanita thought it was an angel choir until she saw it come into sight and the glorious voices rolled forth in a volume of song.

Then the children had breakfast and they made their aguinaldo, for every servant on the place expected a present as surely as did the old darkies of Southern days. The postman, the errand boy, the porter, the sereno who walks the street all night with his lantern, trying your door to see if it is locked properly, and assuring you that all is well as the hours strike, — all must be remembered. Then the señora took the carriage, and the children accompanied her, as she filled it with sweetmeats for the poor children and such of her special protégés as could not come to the house for their aguinaldo.

It was a cold day, for Granada grows cold in the winter time, and is not like other Spanish cities, which have summer all the year. The wind sweeps down from the Sierras and brings with it a blustering hint of mountain snows; and as the houses have no furnaces and seldom good stoves to heat them, even the rich can suffer, and the poor do suffer bitterly.

While the sun shines it matters not, for the sun of Andalusia is so warm and bright that it blesses all who lie beneath it; but when the dark days come or evening's mantle falls upon the town, people hover close about the brazero and long for summer.

With Fernando it mattered little, for he was seldom still enough to be cold, and he spent a merry Christmas, falling asleep to dream of delightful things, and waking to the happy thought that it would soon be the feast of the Circumcision. This is New Year's Day, and is celebrated with much festivity in Spain. The evening before there is a grand party for the grown-ups, and slips of paper are passed around, one being drawn by each person. They are in pairs, so that the one who draws number one must go to supper with number one, and great merriment is made over the pairing off of the guests. The gentleman has to send a bunch of flowers or sweets to the lady whose number he draws, and not a few matches have been made in Spain by this merry custom.

Fernando and Juanita, however, were quite otherwise engaged. They were sent early to bed and were dreaming of the sugar-plums of the morrow, wondering whom they would first meet, for they think in Spain that what happens to you on New Year's Day will determine the course of the whole year. If you meet a pauper you will have bad luck, but if you see a man with gold in his pocket, you will have money all the year.

Merrier still was the feast of the Three Kings, which is the day upon which little Spanish children have gifts made them as American children do at Christmas. This is in honour of the Wise Men having brought presents to Our Lord on that day, so that on the eve of January sixth, the feast of the Epiphany, Fernando and Juanita set their little shoes on their balcony with a wisp of straw to feed the Magi's horses, and with many surmises as to what they would find in them on the morrow. What wonderful things there were! Fernando had all the things that boys love,—tops, marbles, balls, and a fine knife; while Juanita had a wonderful dolly and all manner of dainty things for her to wear. "The Three Kings never make one feel like the governor of Cartagena," said Fernando, as he tossed his new ball and lovingly fingered his knife.

"But there is still another gift for thee and thy sister," said his father, and he led them to the door. There stood a wonderful little donkey, his bridle decorated with streaming ribbons and bells, his kind eyes blinking as he turned his head and seemed to say, "Hello, Little Master, are you and I going to be great friends?"

"Oh, papa, is that for us?" cried Fernando, while Juanita clapped her tiny hands with delight. It took Fernando but a moment to spring on the donkey's back, but his mother cried, warningly:

"Be careful, son! Remember how the little Prince of Granada rode too fast through the streets, and fell from his pony and was killed."

"Have no fear," her husband said, smiling, "the donkey will not go fast enough to hurt him; that is why I selected him." And he placed Juanita up behind her brother, bidding Manuel walk beside them, while Mazo, unbidden, jumped around.

Everything else that Fernando had sank into insignificance when compared to the little donkey, which he named Babieca, and which he and Juanita rode whenever they had a chance. Babieca was a kind little beast, though something of a rogue. He seemed to know that he must play no tricks when Juanita rode him, and he behaved himself well; but when Fernando rode, it was quite another matter. Babieca would prick up his long ears and go along quietly, then stop suddenly without saying "by your leave," and, of course, Fernando would go over his head. He would not hurt himself at all, and the naughty little mule would look at him wonderingly as if to say: "Now what on earth are you doing down there?" Fernando soon grew to expect such antics and was on the lookout for them.

When St. Anthony's Day came, of course Babieca had to go with the other four-footed friends of the saint, to be blessed and insured from all harm through the year. The seventeenth of January is the day of St. Anthony, patron of mules, horses, and donkeys, and a grand parade took place. All the people of the town who had such animals drove them down to the church to be blessed and to get a barley wafer. Many of the animals were gaily decorated with streamers and ribbons, and some with flowers; and all along the streets small booths were set up containing little images of St. Anthony and barley cakes. Babieca behaved very well at his blessing, though his refractory tongue did try to nibble the priest's stole; but some of the horses kicked and neighed, and, with the braying of the many donkeys and mules, there was a din not often heard in staid Granada.

There were no more fêtes for the time being, and Fernando, a trifle spoiled by all the gaiety, had to return to his studies again. It was a long month before carnival time, but his thoughts went forward to that delightful season, and it seemed to the little boy as if it would never come. However, as "all things come to him who will but wait," the great day arrived at last, and Fernando was wild with joy. Carnival time is just before the beginning of Lent, and is a season of great merriment. Under a turquoise sky, with no clouds to mar its fairness, there is a pageant almost like those of the days of chivalry, and Fernando and Juanita, attended by their faithful Manuel and Dolores, saw it all. Fernando dressed as a page, and his sister as a court lady of the days of Isabella the Catholic, and they were masked, as are all the people who throng the streets on these gay days.

Sunday, Monday, and Tuesday the carnival continues, each year, and the children are asked to little dances at the houses of friends, and also to hear student choirs sing and to see plays. But what they most enjoy is mingling in the crowds upon the paseo, throwing confetti at those who throw at them, seeing the flower-decked carriages, the wonderful costumes; monks, nuns, generals, court ladies, flowers, animals, all are represented, — all are laughing and throwingconfetti right and left. Children are selling confetti, crying shrilly, "Confetti, five centimos a packet. Showers of a million colours! Only a perro Chico!"Ah, how gay and delightful it all is! Juanita saw much, and Dolores lay down at night thanking the saints that carnival lasted but three days! But Fernando saw everything, and poor Manuel's legs were weary as he kept pace with his little master, now here, now there, now everywhere, laughing and jesting, the merriest lad in all the carnival.

Alas, it was all over! Ash Wednesday dawned, dull and heavy, the weather as sad and sorry as the day. Fernando dragged himself to church, where his brow was marked with ashes according to custom, and gazed longingly at the Entierro de la sardina, a bit of pork the size and shape of a sardine, buried to show that the fast had begun, for no one in Spain eats meat on Ash Wednesday, and very little of it in Lent.

Fernando looked so depressed at supper that his mother asked him:

"What is the trouble, little son, are you ill?"

"No, mamma," he said. "But it is so long till Easter."

"Not if you do not think about it," said his mother with a smile. "Do your work with a will, and the days will pass quickly. If you are a good boy, you shall have a treat at Easter."

"Oh, what will that be," he asked, and Juanita cried, eagerly, "Shall I have it, too?"

"Both of you," the mother said. "Your father is going to take us to Sevilla, to see the grand Easter festival, and we shall see your brother and sister as well, and your cousins and your Aunt Isabella, so you must be good children."

"Indeed we will," cried both, joyously, at the thought of so much pleasure.

CHAPTER VII.

EASTER IN SEVILLA

EASTER in Sevilla! What a gay and charming time it is! Flowers are everywhere, blooming in beauty, and all the people seem joyous in the thought that the long season of fasting is over.

Fernando and Juanita had arrived in the city on the Saturday before Palm Sunday, and were wild with delight at seeing their cousins, Mariquita, Pepita, and Angel, and in looking forward to the delights of the week's holiday with its processions and fêtes. Beginning with the beautiful Procession of the Palms, on Palm Sunday, all through Holy Week are processions and celebrations, and the little folk thoroughly enjoy them.

Their older brother and sister were there, also, and full of wonderful tales of what they had done at school. Fernando thought Pablo was a wonderful being, and that everything he did was perfect. He could hardly wait until he himself would be big enough to go away to college; and little Juanita felt quite the same way about Augustia, who had learned many things in the convent.

"Indeed, niña," she said, "it is pleasant at school with the girls, but that Mother Justina makes one work so hard, and that the play-hours are few. I have embroidery to make, and lessons to say, and my class learns French as well as Castilian. But the other girls are charming. Most of all I like Paquita de Guiteras, an Americana, at least she comes from the Island of Cuba, and the girls say that she is an Indian, and that her mother was an Indian princess married to her father, a noble Spaniard. Of this I cannot say, and she herself does not relate, but she says that in Cuba the Spaniards have often married the Indians and have been kind to them, and have not destroyed them as have the Americanos in the Estados Unidos. Well, niña, Paquita is the merriest of girls! She has always some prank to play upon some one, and, indeed, she cares not if it is the Mother Superior herself, so she can have her joke. Her aunt, good Sister Mercedes, is always fretting for fear lest Paquita should be in disgrace, but it worries Paquita not at all. One night she did the funniest thing. There is one girl who is very mean to the little ones, always teasing them, and they dare say nothing, as she is the niece of the Mother Superior, and she believes nothing against her. This Teresa Alcantara once found a little girl, and teased her until Paquita could stand it no longer, and flew at Teresa and bit her hand. Sister turned at that moment and saw the bite, but she had not seen what had gone before, and would not listen to what I tried to tell her, and Paquita is always too proud to try to make excuses, and just looked at Sister so fiercely from her great black eyes that the Sister was still more displeased.

"'Thou art but a savage wildcat,' she said, and took her to Mother Superior for punishment. She could not have any playtime for a whole week, and she would have to apologize to Teresa, too, and I think she hated that the worst of anything. But she got even with her, as you shall hear. She found out that Teresa was terribly afraid of cats, and one night, when we were all safely tucked away in our little beds, there came from behind Teresa's curtains a terrible scream, and she jumped out of bed and rushed up and down the dormitory. Such a breach of decorum was never seen before, and the nuns were shocked to a degree. Teresa kept shrieking, 'A wild beast is in my bed! a wild beast is in my bed!' and after calming her down they went to investigate. What do you think they found? A feather duster! It was tucked under the sheets, and who could have put it there? No one knew, but every one felt that Paquita was the only one who could have thought of such mischief. But the sisters did not try to find out, for one of them had seen Teresa teasing the little girl, and knew why Paquita disliked her so much; and after that the big bully let us little ones alone."

"Oh, it must be so nice," sighed Juanita, but Pablo laughed, and said that those were girl's stories, and that far more exciting things happened at the naval college, especially when they all went on a cruise.

On Easter Sunday morning the children went to the cathedral to see the wonderful dances which take place but three times a year. Fernando and Juanita were struck dumb with the beautiful cathedral, so unlike the Gothic one of Granada; for this one at Sevilla is a Saracenic church, built hundreds of years ago, begun by the Moorish Sultan, Yakub al Mansour, in 1184.

How strange it seemed to see dancing in church! Fernando and Juanita sat beside their mother, on their little camp-stools, for there are no pews in

Spanish churches. The whole centre of the church is empty, and people kneel there during the mass, or if they are too tired or too little to stand, they rent camp-stools for half a cent, and an old woman who has them in charge hobbles along with a stool, which they may keep while the service lasts.

The men generally stand, and it is interesting to see them settle themselves in a comfortable position when the sermon begins, and stand there almost without moving while the preacher speaks, sometimes a half-hour, sometimes a whole hour. But the hearers do not seem to mind, for these Spanish monks are very fine preachers.

As the children gazed at the beautiful altar covered with flowers, there came the sound of music,—violins, flutes, flageolets, and hautboys all making a quaint harmony,—and with the music was mingled the sound of youthful voices, fresh and sweet, and a band of boys entered the chancel, and gliding down the altar steps danced quietly, singing as they danced. Their bodies swayed to and fro in time to the music, at first slowly, then, as the time quickened, castanets click-clicked with the other sounds, and the boys moved faster and faster, still in perfect time, yet not with wild abandon, but rather with dignified respect for the place. They were quaintly dressed in the court costumes of the Middle Ages; on their heads were big Spanish hats, turned up at one side with a sweeping blue feather, a mantle of light blue was over one shoulder, their vests were of white satin, their hose and shoes of white. The boys danced on until the great bells of the Giralda rang out, and then they vanished, the music growing softer and softer, until its last strains sounded far away, like a floating wave of heavenly harmony.

"How pretty the dance was," said little Juanita, as they walked home from the service. "Why do they dance in church?"

"The Holy Scriptures say that David danced before the Lord," her mother answered, "so perhaps that is the reason the Sevillians think this is a form of worship, but you must ask your cousins to tell you how it was first done."

"Do tell me, Mariquita," said the little girl, and her cousin said, "I do not know how it happened at first, but it has been done ever since the Moors were here in Sevilla. Only once in hundreds of years has it been stopped, and then an archbishop said it was not right tohave dancing in church. He made every one very angry, for the people said, 'What our fathers did is good enough for us!' So they went to the Pope, and he said that he could not tell unless he saw the dance. So the boys and the musicians were taken to Rome, and there danced before the Holy Father, who said, 'I see no harm in this, any more than in the children's hosannas before Our Lord when He entered Jerusalem. Let them have their dance so long as the clothes which they wear may last.' Then they came back and so determined were they to continue it for ever, that they never let the clothes wear out to this day. If one piece of a suit shall be worn it is so quickly mended or repaired that no suit has ever worn out all at once, so that these are the same suits as those worn long ago."

"I am so glad they still have it," said Fernando, "for I wouldn't have missed seeing it to-day for anything."

CHAPTER VIII.

RAINY DAYS

"MAMMA, would you allow me to go to the bull-fight with father and Pablo?" asked Fernando next day.

"No, indeed, my son, a bull-fight is no place for women and children," his mother replied. "I have never been to one in all my life, and Juanita shall never attend. I wish Pablo did not care to go, either, but he must do as he wishes now that he is grown. A boy cannot always be at his mother's girdle, but you must be much bigger than now before you will see such a sight."

Fernando sighed, but he knew that there was no use saying more, for the word of la madre was law. He was very anxious to see abull-fight, for every boy in Spain desires that above all things. The fights are held on all holidays, but the finest one of all is at Easter. The immense amphitheatre of Sevilla holds thousands of spectators, men wild with excitement over the sport, and even women, though the most refined ladies do not frequent the corridos. The bull is turned loose in the centre of the huge ring and tormented until he is ready to fight. Men with sharp-pointed darts, called banderillos, tease him by throwing their barbs at him, and pricking his skin until he is nearly crazy. Then men mounted on horseback, the picadores, wave scarlet cloths before his eyes, exciting him still more, for a bull hates red worse than anything in the world. He dashes at the cruel cloth, and sometimes is too quick for the man who carries it, tossing him on his horns, but generally it is the poor horse who is killed, and the man jumps away to safety. The matador is the one who slays the bull, and he is sometimes killed himself. It is a terribly cruel affair, though Spaniards say it is not so cruel as our prize-fighting.

It was late that evening when Fernando went to bed, and ere he did so there was quite an excitement. They were all seated upon the piazza of the house, he and Juanita, his cousins and their elders, when there was a great cry from the street, "The toro! The toro!" and a clatter of horses' hoofs. All screamed loudly, for to have a bull escape from the pens is a frequent occurrence, and not a very pleasant one. The cries became louder, the horses' hoofs beat nearer and nearer, and as in the dusk a figure dashed down the street, the señora, screaming loudly, caught Juanita to her and tried to climb the pillar at her side. She was very stout, and the pillar was very slippery, and she could not climb with one arm, so she slid down as fast as she climbed up, squealing all the time, "A toro, Madre di Dios! a toro!"

Fernando was frightened, too, but he was a brave boy, and he tried his best to push his mother up out of danger, boosting her as she slipped down, but not helping very much, as you might suppose. It seemed to him an hour, but it was only a minute before servants came from the house, and as they did so a horse dashed up before the pillars, and, stopped too hastily by his rider, slid along the stones on his hind feet. On his back was Pablo, waving his sombrero, and crying, "What a corrido! It was glorious! Six bulls to die, and Rosito never in such form! But, madre mia, what is the matter?" as he sprang from his horse and assisted his mother to a seat.

The señora could not speak, but Fernando said, "We thought the noise was a bull escaped, and I was assisting my mother to a height of safety."

Pablo looked at the little figure speaking so gravely, then threw back his head and shouted with laughter, but seeing Fernando's hurt expression, stopped quickly, and said:

"Bravo, little brother, thou art a good knight to care for thy mother and sister!"

"Better than thou!" His mother had regained her voice by this time.

"Thou art still the same Pablo, and will yet be the death of thy poor mother," but Pablo kissed her hand so gallantly, and begged her pardon so amiably, that she quite forgave him.

Next day, alas! it was raining, and it rained so hard all that day, and nearly all of the next, that the children were like little bears in a cage. They played with everything they could think of, but after awhile they grew restless and quarrelled so that the grown-up folk grew nervous, too.

At last, Mariquita's father, gay and charming Uncle Ruy, came to the rescue.

"Who wants to take a trip into the country with me?" he asked, and as each one squealed "I!" he said:

"Of course we can't go, really, but we can make believe, and I shall take you to a hacienda outside the old wall of Sevilla.

"It lies amidst orange and olive groves, and all kinds of flowers, and many of the things we eat come from that very place. Who knows how they pickle olives?"

"Are olives pickled?" asked Juanita, and Mariquita said:

"How queer it seems that all the things we eat have to go through so much before they can be eaten. I did not know that olives had to be pickled."

"Yes, mi niña, and we will play that we are visiting an olive grove, and we can see the way the olives are picked and made ready for food. See, here are the trees, and the fruit is picked from them and placed in baskets. There are two kinds of olives used, green and ripe, the green ones are picked just before they begin to turn soft. These are separated from the others, and the bitter taste is removed by soaking in fresh water for a long time, or some picklers soak them for a shorter time in a solution of potash lye. This softens the skin and extracts all bitterness, but the olives must be soaked in clear water, which is frequently changed to get all the potash off. Then they are placed in weak brine, and afterward in stronger, until they have the salty taste which we like so much. Then they are put in small barrels and taken to the bottling rooms, where they are bottled and labelled for the market."

"How is the oil made?" asked Fernando.

"That is harder to do, but it is very interesting to watch. The fresh olives are carefully picked, dried a little, and then crushed. Old-fashioned stone mills are used to crush the fruit, and the mass is pressed to extract the liquid which contains all the watery juice as well as the oil and pulp."

"What do they do after it is pressed?" asked Fernando.

"They let it stand for a month and the refuse goes to the bottom. Then the oil is poured off and allowed to stand another month, when the process is repeated. After the third time the oil is ready for use. The best oil is made in this way, as it keeps its colour and flavour better by the settling process than when it is filtered.

"In some places the olives are placed on a platform and the millstone is placed over them. This is turned round and round by means of a pole to which a donkey is hitched, and the mass which is turned out is placed in rush baskets, which are put under a press which is screwed down by five or six men, so that the oil is squeezed out, but that is a very old-fashioned way of making oil, and there are better ways now. They still use this, however, when there is a big crop, and they want to get the fruit made into oil as rapidly as possible. Great care must be taken that everything is clean and that the oil does not become rancid, or it will all be spoiled."

"Is everything we eat so interesting?" asked Juanita.

"The things we eat and wear, too," her uncle answered, "and nothing in all Sevilla is more interesting than the way of making silk."

"How is that done?" asked Fernando.

"I am afraid I could not make you understand it all, unless you could go to the silk manufactory, and even then it would be hard for you. But I can tell you about the cocoons, and that is the strangest thing about it. The silkworm was first brought to Europe from India in 530, when monks brought it to the Emperor Justinian. The silkworm is a kind of a caterpillar which feeds on the leaves of the white mulberry-tree, and lays his eggs in a kind of gummy substance on the leaves in the end of June to be hatched out in the following April. The caterpillar is small at first, about a quarter of an inch long, but grows to be three inches in length. By means of a substance in their mouths the silkworms spin out silky strands which form cocoons, each fibre being about eight hundred yards long. When ready for weaving, the cocoons are placed in an oven at a gentle heat which kills the chrysalis so that the silk fibres can be removed and wound."

"How do they get the silk wound? Doesn't it break?" asked Fernando.

"It is rather hard to do," his uncle answered, "but they learn to be very careful, and the cocoon is soaked in warm water which loosens the little filaments. When the cocoons are reeled the first step has been taken, and the reeled silk is called raw silk, from which all silk products are made."

"I wish we could see it all, but perhaps we can sometime when we are here again," said Fernando. "Oh, it has stopped raining!"

"Yes, indeed, and the Guadalquiver has overflowed its banks," said Pablo, coming in at that moment. "There has not been such a freshet for years. Come along with me, Nando, and we will go boating in the streets. I climbed to the top of the Giralda, and the whole country looks like a great sea."

"Oh, may I go with Pablo and see?" cried Fernando, and his mother, with many injunctions to Pablo to take care of him, said "Yes."

They went to the Alcazar gardens, those most wonderful gardens of Spain, and as it was early spring the flowers and insects were making merry in the sunshine, which had come back with renewed force, after its vacation. Scarcely tumbled by the rain, lovely banksia roses were climbing over the walls, the rosy, blossoming judas-trees, tinted acacias, and pink almonds were in bloom, and orange-trees were bursting into fragrant beauty. Violets and tulips, yellow oxalis, wild hyacinths, and the scarlet dragon-flower carpeted the ground, while tall white lilies, like fair maidens, and stately iris with sword-like leaves, reminding one of the knights of chivalry who once walked these paths, stood sentinel adown the walks. Fernando saw, too, the insects which flitted among the branches, beetles with bright green coats like emeralds, white and gold butterflies, birds with brilliant wings and sweet voices. But Pablo was thinking more of sport than of nature, and he hurried along until they found a man and a boat to row them, and what a gay sail they had right down the main streets of the town! Past the cathedral steps and the Golden Tower where Columbus piled up gold brought from the New World, Sevillians say, and all the other interesting sights of the city, so that Fernando came home tired and happy, to tell Juanita of the wonderful things he had seen.

"I do not wonder that they say, 'He whom God loves has a house in Sevilla,'" he said. "It is so beautiful a city."

"Truly,—

"'Quien no ha vista Sevilla

No ha vista un maravillo.'"

said Mariquita boastingly, but little Juanita prattled in reply the Grenadino's favourite response—

"'Quien no ha vista Grenada

No ha vista nada.'"

CHAPTER IX

TO THE COUNTRY

HOME again! At first it seemed to Fernando as if he could never go back to school, for after his week of fêtes and processions and fun, lessons were dull things, but he soon fell into the old ways, and there were so many pleasant things at home that he did not pine for Sevilla at all.

He had a pet lamb—what boy has not in spring-time in Spain?—and he was devoted to it for awhile, trying to feed it all manner of things.

"Manuel," he said one day, "I do not know what is wrong with my pet lamb. It will not eat the things I give it. I have never seen so stubborn a thing. Mazo is far different. It will eat anything at all, but the lamb stands and stares at me, and shuts its mouth, no matter what I offer him."

"Lambs are always stubborn," said Manuel. "They do not eat much but milk when they are so young. But here, I have a new kite; will you fly it?"

"Indeed I will," cried the boy, and in an instant the lamb was forgotten, and he was skipping down the street, his kite skimming the air like a gaily coloured bird.

It was a beautiful spring in Granada, and Fernando spent every minute out of doors unless actually compelled to be in school or in bed. The family ate in the lovely patio where the flowers were beginning to blossom, and the sun was not too warm to do without the awning, which in summer stretched overhead. If it was not kites in which he was interested, it was marbles and ball, or even a play bull-fight; and Fernando was very proud when he was chosen to be "toro," and put his head in a basketwork affair with points like horns, and the boys chased him with sticks, running, jumping, and dodging when he turned and charged them as he had heard that the bulls did at the real corridos.

Best of all, it was time to have his head shaved, and of all things that was what he liked. His mother mourned, for the boy's hair was naturally curly, and in winter was as soft and pretty as black velvet. But all Spanish boys have their heads shaved in summer, and Fernando must be like the rest. It was cut so close that it made him look very funny, and his great black eyes shone like beads in his lean brown face, with no soft hair to soften its harsh outlines.

Fernando and Antonio were still devoted friends. They played together after school and on the holidays, and many delightful times did the two boys have, either in the Alhambra or at Fernando's home, where there were many city sights as interesting to Antonio as the delights of the old palace were to Fernando.

So devoted had they become that Fernando felt very sorry to leave his friend when the time came for him to accompany his mother and sister to their country home. Generally he had been delighted to go to the hacienda, and enjoyed the country school even more than the one he attended in the city, but this year he felt so badly over it that his father said:

"Never mind, my son. I shall bring Antonio out to visit you when school is over, and you may have a fine time together at thehacienda." This made Fernando more contented, and he went away with his parents quite happily.

As they started for the country on a bright May day, Juanita said, "Oh, mamma, see that strange cow! It is all dressed with flower-wreaths, and has bells around its neck and flowers on its horns. Why does that young girl lead it, and that old blind man walk behind, and blow that horn and beat the drum?"

"That is a cow to be won in a lottery," said the señora. "Manuel, stop; I wish to buy a ticket. How we Spaniards do love a game of chance! See, I shall buy a ticket for each one of you, and maybe your number will win the prize."

"Oh, thank you, mamma!" both children cried, for neither had ever had a lottery ticket before.

"Now I wish you to stop at a cigar-store, and buy a stamp for my letter to your Aunt Isabella, and then we will drive on."

As they turned into the main street leading to the Alameda, Juanita asked, "Oh, mi madre, what are those people sitting in the streets making?"

"Haven't you seen the ice-cream makers before?" said the señora. "No, I think you cannot remember last summer, can you? The gipsies go up to the Sierras in the very early morning, and get donkey-loads of snow, and the people make ice-cream in those pails with the snow in it. They sit right at their doors on the sidewalk and make the fresh cream, and any one can buy a glass of it."

"Do let us have some," cried the children, and their indulgent mother ordered the horses stopped while they ate some of the delicious fresh cream.

As the carriage rolled on down the steep street, so narrow that as Manuel said "one can hardly pass another after a full dinner," the swineherd was just coming out for the day, and Juanita cried:

"Oh, madre! See that man with the pipe in his mouth; what queer music he plays! What is he?"

"He is the swineherd, niña. See, he comes from his alley, staff in hand," the señora said. "Watch him blow his pipe without turning his head, and the pigs come after him, as if he had charmed them. Little and big, dark and light, fat and scrawny, there they come following him to pasture. Every alley we pass adds some curly tail to the procession. Now he is ready to turn out of the town into that grove, and see what an army of piggies follows him! He never looks for any of them, but they hear the music of his pipe and start because they learned long ago that it leads them to good pastures."

"I think they are too funny for anything," said the little girl. "Does he bring them back at night?"

"Yes, and every little piggy knows his own alley, and goes right home with a little frisk of his curly tail to say 'good night,'" said her mother, smiling.

"See those oxen; are they not splendid fellows? I love to see them draw their loads so easily. Beautiful creamy creatures, with their dark points and their great, soft eyes."

"What is that wooden thing over their heads?" asked Juanita.

"That is the yoke to couple them together. They are the gentlest animals in the world, these great, hornèd beasts, and the driver walks in front of them with a stick over his shoulder, which he seldom thinks of using."

"Oh, what a cunning little donkey!" cried the little girl, as they passed a tiny donkey laden with panniers filled with flowers, fruit, vegetables, bread, fowls, and even a water-jar. "How prettily he is clipped, all in a pattern."

"Mamma," said Fernando, "some of the donkeys that the gipsies have clipped have mottoes and pictures on them. I know a boy whose donkey has 'Viva mi Amo' on his side. I don't like that, for if the donkey doesn't love his master, it is telling a story."

His mother laughed. "We will hope he has a good little master, and then the donkey will care for him and not be telling a falsehood with his fur.

"But here we are almost to the hacienda, and how short the ride has seemed. Now if two children I know are good, we shall have a delightful summer, and although you are to be in the country, and thou, Fernando, will go to a country school, remember the saying of thy fathers:

"'Quando fueres par despoblado

Non hagas desaquisado,

Porque quando fueres per poblado

Iras a lo vesado.'"

CHAPTER X.

GAMES AND SPORTS

THE hacienda was more beautiful than it had been in the fall, and Fernando was soon busy as a bee. He had of course to attend school, but it was a country school, not so strict nor so large as the city one, and he enjoyed showing off his superior accomplishments to the other boys. This the others did not relish, and there was a grand fight to see which was the strongest, and when Fernando had whipped all the boys of his own size, he was happy and felt that he had not disgraced the name of Guzman. Manuel did not attend him in the country, and Fernando much enjoyed doing as he liked, roaming about, taking his own time to come home, tramping about the orange groves, or sailing boats in the brook.

When school was over and Antonio came for the promised visit, what merry times there were! The boys went swimming at all hours. They ran bareheaded all over the place, Mazo after them, their constant companion. Fernando had a few lessons to do each morning, a master to teach him his French, music, and drawing,—for boys of his class in Spain are accomplished as well as educated,—but these were soon over, and then, stung by the bees, burnt by the sun, wet by the rain, eating green oranges, doing in fact what American boys, or boys all over the world will do if let alone, this was the way in which the two Spanish boys spent their vacation.

Juanita, meantime, was having a very happy time. She, too, had a few lessons, and her aya was giving place to a governess, but she was still too young to learn much, and the beautiful out-of-doors was a great lesson-book to her. Riding Babieca, tagging after the boys, sun-tanned and rosy, she grew strong and hearty, and was never so happy as when allowed to go with her brother and Antonio. Generally they took very good care of her, and her mother felt that she was safe with the two boys. Fernando teased her a good deal, but Antonio was of a calmer mood, and was always her gentle knight.

All manner of games were played by these happy children, who, with their little neighbours of the nearest hacienda, made a merry group. They were simple-hearted little folk, and the boys had not reached the state described in the old Spanish rhyme of the boys of Madrid:

"They should be romping with us,

For they are only children yet;

But they will not play at anything

Except a cigarette.

No plays will cheer the Prado

In future times, for then

The little boys of seven

Will all be married men."

Fernando, and even the graver Antonio, entered into all the childish sports with the rest, and an especial favourite was a play very much like our "London Bridge is Falling Down," called the "Gate of Alcala." Two children are chosen to head the lines, and called Rose and Pink. They form an arch with their arms held up and their fingers locked, and under this the other children pass headed by the mother. They sing gaily a little dialogue:

The last child, with squeals of delight, is caught in the falling arms, and chooses whether she shall follow Rose or Pink, taking herplace behind the one of her choice. When all have been chosen, there is a grand tug of war, the merry party singing, meantime.

The boys enjoyed playing soldier, and would whittle toy swords out of sticks, and form in line, marching and singing:

"The Catalans are coming,

Marching two by two;

All who hear their drumming,

Tiptoe for a view,

Aye, aye, tiptoe for a view;

Red and yellow banners,

Pennies very few.

Aye, aye, pennies very few.

"Red and yellow banners

The moon comes out to see;

If moons had better manners

She'd take me on her knee.

Aye, aye, she'd take me on her knee.

She peeps through purple shutters;

Would I were tall as she.

Aye, aye, would I were tall as she.

"Soldiers need not learn letters

Nor any schooly thing;

But, unless they mind their betters,

In golden chains they swing.

Aye, aye, in golden chains they'll swing.

Or sit in silver fetters,

Presents from the king.

Aye, aye, presents from the king."

The prettiest of all the games is that of the "Little White Pigeons," which all Andalusian children love to play. The little companions form in two rows, and, facing each other, dance forward and slip beneath the upraised arms of the opposite side. Thus they pass under the "Silver Arches" to Sevilla and Granada:

"Little white pigeons are dreaming of Seville,

Sun in the palm-trees, rose and revel.

Lift up the arches, gold as the weather,

Little white pigeons come flying together.

"Little white pigeons, dream of Granada,

Glistening snows on Sierra Nevada.

Lift up the arches, silver as fountains,

Little white pigeons fly to the mountains."

Our little Spanish cousins play nearly all the same games that American children play, only their "Blind Man's Buff" is called "Blind Hen," and "Pussy Wants a Corner," is called "Cottage to Rent," and played with the rhyme:

"Cottage to rent, try the other side,

You see this one is occupied."

Their game of tag is called the "Moon and the Morning Stars," and is played by one child being chosen as the Moon and forced to keep within the shadow. The rest of the children, being Morning Stars, are safe only where it is light. If the Moon can catch a Star in the shadow, the Star must become a Moon, and as the Stars scamper in and out of the shadow, all sing:

"O the Moon and the Morning Stars,

O the Moon and the Morning Stars,

Who dares to tread — oh

Within the shadow."

"Hide and Seek" the children played, and "Forfeits," and all manner of other games, and as the sun nearly always shines in Andalusia, the summer was one long merry round of out-of-door fun.

CHAPTER XI.

A TERTULIA

SEPTEMBER found the children at home again, and Fernando back at school, while Juanita had a governess for a part of each day, though she was not expected to learn a great deal; for the Spaniards think if their girls are sweet and gentle they need not be very learned. If a Spanish girl of sixteen knows how to read and write, simple arithmetic, a little history, and can dance and embroider well, she is quite accomplished enough to marry, which is what most of them intend to do.

Things were going very quietly, when there came an excitement so great for the children that they were almost wild. This was the home-coming, in the latter part of September, of Pablo, just in from his long summer cruise, with a fortnight's leave of absence. He came home to celebrate his coming of age, and there was to be a tertulia in his honour. The children were to stay up to the party, and as it was the first time that they had been permitted to stay up after eight o'clock, they were delighted. To them it was the greatest event in their lives, and they were almost afraid to breathe all day, for fear the treat would be cut off. Juanita even stood quite still to have her curls made, which was generally a performance attended with agony, and before the end of which her aya was sure to say, "Hush, Mambru will certainly get you!" Mambru is to a little Spanish girl what a bogey is to an American child, and she will be very good for fear of Mambru. But the day passed off pleasantly, and the children were dressed and sent down to the patio to await the arrival of the guests.

The pleasant thing about a Spanish party is that there is no fuss made, and therefore everybody enjoys themselves. The hostess never tires herself out preparing for her guests so that she cannot be cheerful and agreeable when they arrive. The hospitality of Spain is perfect. A Spaniard gives his friends just what is good enough for himself, and never thinks of doing more. So there was not a great brewing and baking on the day of the party, and flushed, heated faces; but there were a few simple refreshments, much pleasant talk and hearty laughter among old and young. There were about thirty friends of the family who came in to talk and chat. The parents came with their daughters, for girls never go to parties alone in Spain, and old and young spent the evening together. Some one played on the piano and the young people danced, lovely Trinidad del Aguistanado dancing with Pablo. This Juanita watched with delight. Trinidad was the loveliest of all the girls, and she thought, of course, Pablo should have the prettiest maiden in all the world. She was as sweet as she was pretty, and said to the little girl:

"What is thy name, niña?" and when Juanita answered, sweetly:

"Juanita, to serve God and you," as all Spanish children are taught to answer, Trinidad kissed her on both cheeks, and gave her a rose from her girdle. At this Juanita was delighted, and Pablo sighed prodigiously. The older people, too, seemed well pleased with Pablo's choice, for the girl's family was as good as theirs, and the two had been friends for many years.

"Juanita," said Fernando in a whisper, "I believe that Pablo will bite the iron of the Señorita Trinidad. Will it not be strange tothink of him beneath her window, singing of love to his guitar?"

"It will be beautiful," sighed the little girl, for Spanish children are always interested in the love affairs of their older brothers and sisters, and even little girls talk about them. "How handsome Pablo looks as he talks with her."

"They are as fair as the lovers of Teruel," said old Dolores, who was at the party to take care of her little charges.

"Tell us about them," said Juanita, eagerly, for she dearly loved Dolores's quaint stories; and the aya began:

"In the town of Teruel there lived, many years ago, a Spanish knight, Don Juan Diego Martinez de Marcilla, and he loved with all his heart Doña Isabel de Segura. Alas, unhappily! for the fathers of the two lovers were enemies, and would not listen to love between them.

"'Thou art but a second son,' said Don Pedro de Segura, the father of Doña Isabel. 'Moreover, thou hast not a fortune equal to that of my daughter, who possesses thirty thousand sueldos in good gold, and is my sole heiress.'

"'Full well I know that I am in no wise worthy of thy fair daughter,' said Don Juan, 'and upon her grace have I no claim save that she loves my unworthy self. But since this is God's truth, I pray you give me the chance to prove my devotion, and I will furnish sufficient fortune to equal hers. I go to the wars with my lord, King Sancho of Navarre. Grant me five years in which to gain this fortune, and give me your promise that for that length of time you will not force Doña Isabel to marry another.'

"Doña Isabel was very young, and her father very fond, and by this he could keep her with him five long years, and, moreover, marry her to whom he pleased, for he said to himself, 'In that time both of them will forget,' and so he smilingly said:

"'Your words have some reason. Go with God, and if you return, well and good. My daughter shall not marry against her will for five years to this day, but mark me, rash youth, not one day more shall she wait.'

"Then the lovers bade each other farewell, and Don Juan rode to the wars. These were waged against the wicked Moors, and with knights and squires, the armies of Don Alphonso of Castile, Don Pedro of Aragon, and Don Sancho of Navarre fought long and fiercely until, at the great battle of Las Navas de Tolosa, the Moor was crushed. Many a valiant deed was done, and Don Juan was bravest of them all. He broke through the chain which guarded the tent of the Moorish king, and thereby gained great glory and won for himself the right to wear a chain around the margin of his shield in honour of the day. He gained great renown and fortune, but, alas, he was sorely wounded, and it was more than five years before he could return to his beloved. He arrived in Teruel but one short day after the time was up, and found Doña Isabel married to another, Don Pedro Fernandez de Azagra. Despairing, he desired to see his beloved once more, and climbed to her window on her wedding-night. Finding her alone and her husband sleeping, he implored her to give him one last kiss. She refused, and said, weeping, 'Alas! you came not and I thought myself forgotten. I am wedded to this good man, and to him alone belong my caresses.'

"At this his heart broke, and crying, 'Farewell, beloved!' he dropped dead at her feet.

"At that moment her husband awoke, and she told him straightway the truth, at which he said, 'Thou hast been cruel and unkind to this good man, but to me faithful and true, and I shall but love thee the more!' and he took the body of the poor Don Juan and bore it secretly to his father's step and laid it down and fled away.

"When the body of the knight was found, there was great mourning, and he was given a grand funeral at the cathedral, to which all Teruel came to do him honour. There also came the unhappy Doña Isabel, disguised so that none might know her, and, determined to give her lover in death the kiss which she had denied him in life, she stooped to kiss his lips. Lo! the eyes unclosed, he smiled at her, and they closed again, and she fell beside him dead! All were struck dumb with horror, but Don Azagra came forward and told the mournful story, whereupon the two bodies were buried in the same grave.

"'Separated in life, in death they shall be together,' said the generous knight who had been her husband but not her beloved; and this is the sad, sad story of the lovers of Teruel."

"Oh, thank you, Dolores, it is a beautiful story," cried Juanita, and the young people who had gathered around to hear clapped their hands, and thanked her, too.

"What think you, Señorita Trinidad, would you have kissed your lover had you been Doña Isabel?" asked Pablo of the young girl.

"I should not have married the other man, señor," she said, flushing prettily.

"Come, Trinidad, you must sing for us," cried one of her friends. "Sing the song of Santa Rita," and Trinidad, with a merry little glance at Pablo, sang the gay little song which Spanish girls sing in jest, asking Santa Rita to procure them a good husband.

"Santa Rita, Santa Rita,

Cada una de nosotros necesita,

Para uso de diario

Un marido milionario,

Anunque sea un animal

Si tal, si tal, si tal, si tal,

Un marido milionario,

Anunque sea un animal."

Everybody applauded loudly, and Trinidad, laughing and blushing, sang again. The older people sat about serenely, some talking, others playing cards or dominoes. The younger ones played sprightly games and talked like magpies, and the children listened spellbound.

"Who art thou, Pablo?" laughed one, and Pablo answered, merrily:

"Ole Saltero, sin vanidad,

Soy muy bonito, soy muy sala!"

And every one laughed, and Trinidad gave him a charming glance from under her black lashes.

Refreshments were passed around, very simple ones. There were trays of water, and by each glass round lumps of sugar, which the guests dipped in the water and ate, hard little cakes, cups of thick chocolate into which finger cakes were dipped and eaten, and some charming little bonbons. There was no wine, for although the finest wine in the world is made in Spain, the Spaniards are great water drinkers, and seldom have wine except at dinners. The men all smoked, but not the ladies, for while the Mexican women sometimes smoke a dainty cigarrillo, Spanish women do not.

Later on, Pablo's health was drunk in tiny glasses of sherry, as this was a special occasion, and pleasant speeches were made to him, wishing him all success in his career.

"Thou art now a man, my son," said his father, proudly and affectionately. "Remember that since the time of the Emperor Charles V., thy fathers have had the right to wear the Golden Key upon their hip, and do nothing to disgrace thy name. On the sword of my grandfather was engraved the motto, 'Do not draw me without reason nor sheathe me without honour!' Let his motto be thine own, and remember that to a Spaniard honour comes first."

Then the party broke up, and Fernando and Juanita were trotted off to bed, and sleepily murmured their evening prayer:

"Jesus, Joseph, Mary,

Your little servant keep,

And with your kind permission,

I'll lay me down to sleep!"

and they heard through the soft moonlight the tinkle of Pablo's guitar, as he strolled along to bite the iron beneath the grating of the dainty Señorita Trinidad.

CHAPTER XII.

VIVA EL REY!

ALL Granada was in a flutter! It was the brightest of October days, and the sun seemed to be trying to be as bright as the people, or the people to be as gay as the sunshine. Fernando and Juanita hopped out of bed and ran to the window the first minute they were awake, and squealed with delight when they saw that the day was fair.

"Oh, mamma!" cried Fernando. "Is it not glorious? The fête will be a success!" and Juanita echoed her brother, "Is it not wonderfully fair!"

"Come and have your chocolate quickly, like good children," returned their mother, "for you must be ready early."

As soon as the children were breakfasted, they were dressed in their best clothes, Juanita all in white, with a gay sash, and Fernando in a sailor suit of blue, and they waited impatiently for their parents to be ready to start for the fête.

It was a great day for Granada, for the king was coming to visit the city, and it had been many years since royalty had honoured the Andalusian town. Spaniards are nearly always devoted to their king, and in Andalusia there are very few who are not fond and proud of the young King Alphonso.

In Northern Spain there are many who are called Carlists, and who believe that the descendants of Don Carlos are the lawful kings of Spain, and these have often gotten up revolutions and tried to set their own favourites up as kings.

In Barcelona and some of the eastern provinces there are many who like neither King Alphonso nor Don Carlos, and these are anarchists; but Granada was heart and soul for the king, and all the people were overjoyed at his coming.

Every balcony in the city was covered with flowers; flags and banners floated everywhere. The Alameda was ablaze with decorations, and every face wore a smile of welcome. The programme for the day was a simple one. The king was to be met at the station by a delegation, a band, and a mounted escort, witness a military review on the Alameda, and depart by an afternoon train. All Granada must see him, and Fernando and Juanita with it.

It had been decided that the best time for the children to have a good look at the king was when he drove to the Alhambra, and Manuel and Dolores started early to take them to meet Antonio, who had promised to provide places within the Alhambra grounds, where the general multitude would be less likely to go, and where the children would have a finer view. Pablo went with them, for he was still at home, and he walked beside Babieca to see that Juanita did not fall off, on her long ride up-hill.

"See there, little sister," he said. "Is not that an easy way to get milk for the day?"

The goatherd was passing at the head of his procession of goats, looking neither to the right nor to the left, expecting his herd to follow him as gravely as he walked; but a peasant woman stole out of her door, and quietly milked one of the little beasts, who seemed not to object in the least, and took it so calmly that Pablo added, "That is not the first time there has been stolen milk for breakfast, I'm sure."

"See the poor beggar; do give him something, Pablo," said Juanita, touched by a wretched specimen of humanity who sat with blind eyes peering up at them as they passed. Pablo threw a perro chico into the beggar's outstretched hand, but he said:

"You must not be too sad for all the beggars, niña; there is an old rhyme:

"'The armless man has written a letter,

The blind man finds the writing clear;

The mute is reading it aloud,

And the deaf man runs to hear.'

They are not all so sad as they look, but one must give for fear one may slight the really needy."

"Oh, Pablo, may we have some horchata?" cried Fernando, and his brother stopped to purchase some of the snowy, chilly, puckery stuff, and they enjoyed it greatly. Fernando ate too hastily, and his brother said:

"Quita, quita! You must not act so! You are as bad as the king when he was a baby and put his knife in his mouth. His governess said to him, 'Kings do not eat with their knives,' and he haughtily replied, 'This king does!'"

"Indeed," said Fernando, pertly, "the king is my cousin, so it says in my history book that all Spaniards may say."

"He is your cousin, that is, you must love him as your own blood; but say, rather, 'All equal below the king,' and put him ever first. Remember that your fathers have died for the Kings of Spain, and we may have a chance to show our loyalty yet," and Pablo's bright face clouded a moment.

"Listen to the music; there goes the military salute! The king has come, and by the time we reach the Alhambra he will be on his way hither. Get up, Babieca," and he hurried the little donkey along until they reached the top of the hill and found Antonio waiting for them, his face flushed and eager.

"He will pass here," he cried, "beneath the Gate of Justice, and my father says we may stand just behind the guard upon the wall; there could not be a better place."

"How nice that will be!" cried Juanita. "And where is Pepita?"

"There, awaiting you," Antonio answered. "I will take care of Babieca and return," and he led the donkey away, coming back in a few moments, and they all waited impatiently.

Spaniards all love a spectacle, and the young folk could hardly restrain themselves as they heard the strains of music coming nearer and nearer. At last the cavalcade came in sight,—first a troop of soldiers, then a band playing the Marcha Real, then a mounted guard keeping close to His Majesty's carriage. There he sat, the young king, a tall, slight youth, with a pale, proud face and great black eyes, sad, yet merry and tender; a patrician face in every feature, yet a lovable one, and one to arouse all of love and loyalty in his subjects, as the character of Alphonso XIII. arouses their respect and affection.

As the carriage paused at the entrance gate, the king looked up at the eager little group upon the wall and smiled. Juanita and Pepita flung into his carriage their huge bouquets of flowers and to the girls he threw a kiss; but Fernando and Antonio stood up very straight and saluted gravely, and with a smile in his eyes, but with grave lips, the young king raised his hand to his hat and gave them in return the military salute. Then his carriage passed on, and bore him out of sight, but a shout went up from every voice, "Viva el rey!"

"When I grow up I shall be a nun and pray all the time for the king!" said Pepita.

"I shall be a soldier and fight for him," said Fernando, proudly.

"And I," said Juanita, "shall marry and have many children to fight and pray for him and for Spain!"

"Indeed, little sister, perhaps thou hast chosen the better part," said Pablo, laughing heartily.

"See!" cried Antonio, "there goes the carriage again, and hear how the people shout!" and as the bravas rent the air, the children shouted, too:

"Viva Espagna! Viva el rey! Dios guarda usted!"

THE END.